Billy the Bird

To Anthony

From Mrs. Lambert

DICK KING-SMITH

Billy the Bird

Illustrated by

Susie Jenkin-Pearce

SCHOLASTIC INC.

New York Toronto London Auckland Sydney
Mexico City New Delhi Hong Kong Buenos Aires

ISBN 0-439-37541-X

Text copyright © 2001 by Dick King-Smith.
Illustrations copyright © 2001 by Susie Jenkin-Pearce.
All rights reserved.
Published by Scholastic Inc., 555 Broadway, New York, NY 10012,
by arrangement with Hyperion Books for Children,
an imprint of Disney Children's Book Group, LLC.
SCHOLASTIC and associated logos are trademarks and/or
registered trademarks of Scholastic Inc.

12 11 10 9 8 7 6 5 4 3 2 1   2 3 4 5 6 7/0

Printed in the U.S.A.   40

First Scholastic printing, February 2002

This book is set in 13.5-point Life Roman.
The artwork for each illustration was prepard using pencil.

Other books by Dick King-Smith

ACE: *The Very Important Pig*
Babe: *The Gallant Pig*
The Cuckoo Child
Dick King-Smith's Animal Friends:
Thirty-one True Life Stories
Godhanger
Harriet's Hare
Harry's Mad
I Love Guinea Pigs
The Invisible Dog
Jenius: *The Amazing Guinea Pig*
Martin's Mice
The Merman
Mixed-up Max
A Mouse Called Wolf
Mr. Ape
Mr. Potter's Pet
Mysterious Ms. Slade
Paddy's Pot of Gold
Pigs Might Fly
Puppy Love
The Robber Boy

Billy the Bird

One

I was four, nearly five, when my brother, Billy, was born. I was so excited. I had been longing for a baby brother, or sister, I didn't care which.

Dad said he'd really like a son. Mom said she didn't care: another daughter would be just as nice. Both of them said it didn't matter which it was, as long as it was a normal, healthy, happy baby. Which is just what Billy appeared to be. But neither of them had the faintest idea (and they still don't) that though Billy was (and still is) healthy and happy, he was definitely not normal.

I didn't find out till he was four and I was eight, nearly nine.

It was a warm summer evening, Friday, June 20, in fact—a date I will never forget. I had said good night to Mom and Dad and gone upstairs, and on my way to my bedroom I peeped into Billy's, as I always did, just to see that he was all right. His bed was empty.

At first I wasn't too worried. He must have gone to the bathroom, I thought. But he wasn't in the bathroom, or in Mom and Dad's room, or anywhere else. He must be sleepwalking, I thought; I must go and tell them. But first I had another look in Billy's room in case he'd come back from his sleepwalk. But the bed was still empty.

Then suddenly I heard, above my head, a small snore. I looked up, and there I saw Billy—his knees curled up and his arms wrapped around them. He wasn't walking in his sleep, he was floating in it!

You must have seen pictures on TV of astronauts inside their spacecraft, in orbit beyond Earth's atmosphere, floating around, light as feathers.

You must have thought what fun it would be, to be able to do that. But of course, because of the pull of gravity, it's not possible, down here on Earth, for anyone to become weightless. Not possible, that is to say, for any normal person.

I remember staring up at my little brother with my mouth wide open, like a fish.

I remember the pajamas he was wearing, blue ones with a pattern of pink rabbits.

I remember thinking, thank goodness for the ceiling, otherwise who knows how high he might have gone.

I remember closing the window very quietly in case he might float out through it, and seeing, as I did, that the moon had just risen, and that it was a full moon, huge and round and creamy.

I turned back from the window to see my little

brother dropping back down again, fat arms and legs spread like a starfish, and landing softly on his bed, still fast asleep.

I must tell Mom and Dad, I thought, and then I thought, no, I won't, I'm going to keep it a secret. For one thing's certain, I said to myself: there may be millions of girls called Mary, and probably thousands of Marys that have little brothers called Billy. But I bet I'm the only girl in the world who has a brother who is able to become weightless.

Two

Next morning I talked the whole thing over with my guinea pig, Mr. Keylock. He's named after the man who owns the grocery store where we buy carrots and other stuff for him. Both of them have big red mustaches. People say that animals can't talk. That's not true, lots of them can, and guinea pigs are especially chatty. You've just got to learn all the different languages.

I was so anxious to get Mr. Keylock's opinion about what had happened that I didn't feed him right away, as I usually do. I wanted to know what he thought. I was sure I would understand whatever he would say. You nearly always can if you take the time to listen to animals properly.

Now, for example, when I spoke to him, he chattered back at me, and I was pretty sure I knew what he was saying.

"Do you know what Billy did last evening?" I asked Mr. Keylock.

"No," he said.

"He flew up to the ceiling!"

"Oh."

"Don't you think that's extraordinary?"

"Yes."

"D'you think I should tell Mom and Dad?"

"Up to you."

What's the matter with Mr. Keylock this morning? I thought. He's not saying much. Then I realized. I hadn't fed him yet.

"Would you like a carrot?" I said.

"Yes, yes, yes, yes!" squeaked Mr. Keylock. "I thought you'd never ask."

He gobbled that carrot so greedily that there wasn't much point in saying any more to him till he'd finished.

When he had, I said, "It's kind of a joke, Billy flying, isn't it? Considering his name, I mean." (Our last name is Bird, you see.)

"You must have been dreaming," Mr. Keylock said.

"I wasn't."

"You must have been. Humans can't fly, any more than pigs can. Or guinea pigs."

So I decided to ask Lilyleaf about it.

Lilyleaf is our cat, rather old and very wise. The first thing she said to me when I quizzed her about Billy's flying was "Does he know that he flew?"

"I haven't asked him," I replied.

"Well, don't," said Lilyleaf, "and don't tell him what happened. If he believes he can fly, he'll be jumping out of the window to try it."

So I didn't say anything to my little brother about it. But every evening when I looked into his bedroom, I half expected (half hoped, really) that he'd be floating up against the ceiling. But he never was, not until Sunday, July 20, and this time he wasn't asleep.

As soon as I came into the room, he called down to me from the ceiling.

"Look at me, Mary!" he cried excitedly.

I rushed to shut the window.

Now Billy rolled over and then pulled with his arms and kicked with his legs like a swimmer and flew all around the room.

Just then the cat came in, and Billy called to her, "Look at me, Lilyleaf, I'm flying!" and he turned a somersault in the air. Then he swooped down and landed back on his bed, light as a feather. He put his head on his pillow and shut his eyes and went right back to sleep.

"The first time he flew," said Lilyleaf, "the moon was full, remember?"

"Yes."

"Like now."

"You mean, he can only do it at the full moon?"

"I think so," said Lilyleaf. "It's only then that Billy can defy gravity. When's the next one?"

We went to my room and I looked in the diary that I keep by my bed.

"The next full moon," I said, "will be on Monday, August eighteenth."

"Then that's when he'll fly next," said Lilyleaf.

Usually summer vacation whizzes by, but now the time seemed to go oh so slowly as I waited for Billy's next scheduled flight. I did think again about telling Mom and Dad, but I could just imagine the conversation.

MARY: Mom, Dad, I think I should tell you. Billy can fly.

DAD: Nonsense!

MOM: Don't be silly, darling.

MARY: But he can! Honestly! We saw him, all of us—Lilyleaf, Mr. Keylock, and me.

MOM: You've been dreaming, Mary. Only birds can fly.

DAD (LAUGHING): Don't forget—Billy *is* a bird!

MARY (BECOMING IMPATIENT): But he can, he can!

DAD AND MOM TOGETHER (GETTING ANGRY): Oh, Mary. Don't be silly. You have such an imagination!

So I didn't say anything to them, but at least I could talk about it with the cat and the guinea pig.

Lilyleaf, I was sure, would want to be there when the time came, and so would Mr. Keylock—he made me promise to take him upstairs to watch.

So, at last, on the evening of August 18, the three of us made our way up to Billy's bedroom, and, lo and behold, there he was, already flying around, Billy the Bird!

• 11 •

"Hello, Mary!" he cried. "Hello, Lilyleaf! Hello, Mr. Keylock!" He swooped over our heads.

My heart was thumping. Mr. Keylock's red mustache bristled and Lilyleaf's green eyes glowed as we watched.

We were so fascinated that I quite forgot to close the window, and suddenly Billy flew out through it, and away.

Three

I rushed to the window, carrying my guinea pig, and the cat jumped up on the sill. All three of us stared out to see Billy flying silently away.

Mom and Dad were sitting on the swing seat on the lawn, enjoying the last of the evening warmth. Dad was reading his newspaper; Mom was reading her book. And the full moon was already up.

"Oh, help!" I whispered to Lilyleaf. "I sure hope they don't look up!"

"Neee-o," she said, or that's what it sounded like.

Mom didn't notice, but at that very moment,

just as Billy went swooping over their heads, Dad brushed at a cloud of gnats in front of his face and looked up at the sky.

"Gosh!" he said to Mom. "Did you see that?"

"What?" Mom asked.

"A great big bird just flew over us."

"What was it?" Mom asked.

"Couldn't really see, I was flailing at flies, but it sure was big."

It wasn't, I thought. It was a little Bird.

Just then Mr. Keylock began to squeal loudly, the squeal that I knew meant "Come on, I'm starving, for goodness' sake feed me."

At this Mom and Dad looked up and saw us all at Billy's bedroom window.

"Is Billy asleep?" Mom called.

"Well . . . no," I said.

"Not surprised," said Dad, "considering the racket that greedy animal of yours is making."

"Come on downstairs now, Mary," said Mom. "I'll be up in a minute to say good night to Billy."

Help! I thought. What shall I do? But then I saw Billy coming gliding back over the lawn as silently as an owl, right over the heads of our parents, who were busy talking and, lucky for us, never looked up. Billy swooped in through the window and onto his bed and into it. He lay there grinning at us.

"That was fun, Mary!" he said.

"You gave us all an awful fright," I said. I looked out of the window. Mom was getting up from the swing seat to come into the house. Quickly I bent over Billy's bed.

"Listen," I said to him. "Listen, Billy, this is important. Mom's coming up to say good night, and we're going to have to tell her that you've been flying. If Dad hadn't been distracted just now and seen you, he might have had a heart attack."

But already my little brother was fast asleep, tired out, I guess, by his flight.

Mom came in.

"He's asleep now," I said.

"I would hope so," she said, looking at her watch. "I didn't realize it was so late. Goodness, how time flies."

And that's not the only thing that's been flying, I said to myself.

I didn't sleep very well that night. I lay in my bed, thinking of Mom and Dad sleeping soundly in theirs, and Billy in his. Mr. Keylock would be in the land of dreams, dreams of food, of course, and only Lilyleaf would be awake, hunting out in the dark night.

But every time I was just dropping off, I started to worry. Should I tell Mom and Dad what he'd done? I'd told him we should, but he'd already gone to sleep. I'll tell him again first thing in the morning, I thought. I looked at my watch. One o'clock, morning already!

I must have slept then because when I looked at my watch again it was half past six.

People say that if you have to make a big

decision, it's best to sleep on it first. Well, I had, hadn't I, and now I began to feel different. It looked pretty certain that my little brother could only fly at the time of the full moon, and the next one, my diary said, was not until September 16, twenty-nine days away. No point in telling Mom and Dad yet, was there?

I got out of bed and tiptoed along the passage to Billy's room. Gently, I shook him awake. "I've been thinking," I said. "Perhaps we'd better not tell them."

Billy rubbed his eyes. "Don't know what you mean," he said.

"About your flying."

"Flying?" said Billy. "What do you mean? People can't fly, only birds can."

"But you did! In June and July and again yesterday evening."

"You've been dreaming, silly," said Billy, yawning. "Go away and leave me alone."

After our breakfast I went out into the yard to

Mr. Keylock's hutch, to give him his. Lilyleaf followed.

"Look," I said to them both. "I wasn't dreaming last night, was I? Billy did fly, didn't he?"

"No doubt about it," said the cat.

"And Mr. Keylock, you saw him, too?"

"Yes, yes," said the guinea pig, "and for goodness' sake, girl, don't just stand there holding that carrot, give it here, I'm starving!"

I gave it to him, and Lilyleaf and I watched him digging in to it as if he hadn't been fed for weeks.

"The point is," I said to Lilyleaf, "that this morning I was saying to him that perhaps we shouldn't tell Mom and Dad about it, about him flying, I mean, and he didn't seem to know what I was talking about."

"That figures, Mary," said Lilyleaf. "He can only fly on the night of the full moon, and what's more, only then does he know that he *is* flying. At any other time he's just an ordinary little boy, quite unaware of this gift that he has."

"That must be it!" I said. "Lilyleaf, you *are* clever."

"I know," said the cat in her smug way.

The guinea pig bolted the last of his carrot and squeaked for more in his greedy way.

As we walked back up the garden Lilyleaf said, "Better have a look in your diary."

"Why?" I asked.

"Find out when the next full moon is."

"I know that," I said. "On September sixteenth."

"And what about the other ones, this year?"

"Let's see . . . October sixteenth . . . and then November fourteenth . . . and then December fourteenth."

Four

On September 16, by a stroke of luck, Mom and Dad had some friends over for supper, so there was little risk of their seeing Billy the Bird in action. By the time they had said good-bye to their visitors and come upstairs to make sure my brother was asleep, he was. How amazed they would have been to have heard what he told us when he'd returned.

"That was cool!" he said. "It was wicked! It was awesome!"

"You sound as though you were over the moon," I said.

"No," said Billy. "I didn't go as high as that. But I did fly right up over the town. Our house looked tiny from up there."

"I hope no one looked up and saw you," Lilyleaf said.

"Do you think someone could have seen me?" asked Billy.

"The evenings are still quite light. Someone might have spotted you."

What none of us knew then was that someone had.

The local evening newspaper on September 17 had an article that caught Dad's eye.

"Listen to this," he said to Mom, and he read it aloud.

SIGHTING OF UFO

Several people have reported the sighting of an unidentified flying object high above the town at approximately 8:30 P.M. yesterday evening. It has been variously described as looking like a large bird or a small glider, though some were convinced that the UFO was an alien from another planet. Most unlikely of all was one person's insistence that the figure was a small child. Pigs might fly!

"Honestly!" Dad said. "Some people will believe anything! Of course it was a bird. Probably the same one that flew over last month, remember?"

Later I told Lilyleaf about the article in the newspaper.

"At least it'll be darker next month," I said, "now that winter's coming."

"Better not to open his window till after it's dark," Lilyleaf said. "It would be the safest time, too—your mom and dad will be asleep."

"But how will Billy see his way around?" I said. "Cats can see in the dark, but people can't."

"They can if it's a full moon," said Lilyleaf. "It'll be almost as bright as daylight."

But at both the next two full moons—October 16 and November 14—the weather was cold and very wet, so I kept the window shut, and Billy had to be content with flying around the room, until I hit on the idea of opening his door and letting him fly down the hallway and around Mom and Dad's room and my room and the bathroom, to make the trip more interesting for him. Lilyleaf stood guard at the head of the stairs to give warning in case Mom or Dad came out into the hall below. They did come out, once, during the November flight, and the cat gave a loud "Meow!" and Billy came skimming back down the hallway at top speed and into bed.

"What was Lilyleaf making that noise for?" they said when they came up.

"She wants her supper, I guess," I said.

"I want mine!" squealed Mr. Keylock. "I'm starving!"

"Put that creature back in its hutch, Mary," Dad said. "It'll wake Billy."

"It won't," I said, because I'd seen my little brother's eyelids flicker, and I knew that this time he wasn't asleep, just pretending. When Mom and Dad had gone back downstairs, I whispered to him, "Good boy, you didn't tell them."

"Tell them what?" Billy said.

"That you can fly."

"Of course I didn't," he said. "It's a secret between you and me and Lilyleaf and Mr. Keylock," and he shut his eyes again and fell fast asleep.

But when I said to him the next morning, "Gosh you're getting fast, Billy! You flew along the passage like a swallow!" he only said, "Oh you and your silly dreams."

Five

December 14 was a Sunday, so Dad was at home, and Mom made him start on the Christmas decorations. He grumbled, saying there was loads of time, another eleven days to go.

But in fact he kind of enjoys fixing up all the twinkling lights (he's a real do-it-yourselfer), not just on the Christmas tree but all over the front of our house, too. There's no mistaking the Birds' nest at Christmastime—it's far and away the brightest on the whole street.

Once it was dark, Dad turned all the lights on—just to make sure they were working—and they werc. They looked lovely, all different colors, with some that winked and blinked, and one set—bigger, golden ones—that spelled out MERRY CHRISTMAS. Of course there was a very big golden light up in the sky too, the full moon, and I suddenly thought, oh help, what if Billy just takes off now, in front of everyonc!

But in fact he went to bed and right to sleep, and when it was my bedtime he was still soundly asleep. So I made sure his window was closed, and I drew the curtains to keep out the moon's bright light, and then I shut his bedroom door, leaving Lilyleaf on guard outside it.

"Wake me up if you hcar him moving," I said to her.

Perhaps he won't fly tonight, I thought to myself as I was drifting off, perhaps he doesn't fly every full moon, perhaps he's lost the knack of it. But the next thing I knew was someone saying "Pssssst" in my ear.

"I can hear him," Lilyleaf said. "He has liftoff."

We found Billy doing warm-up circuits of the room.

"Quiet, Billy," I whispered to him. "We don't want to wake up Mom and Dad"; and then I put some warm clothes on him over his pajamas (it was December, after all) and went to open the window.

"Don't be too long," I said to Billy the Bird, "and try not to let anybody see you."

We sat waiting by the window. I was yawning like mad, longing to go back to sleep, but Lilyleaf, being a creature of the night, was wide awake. Just as I was dozing off, she went "Pssssst" in my ear again.

"Here he comes," she said, and in sailed my little brother.

"Good flight?" I said.

"Awesome," said Billy.

"Anyone see you?"

"No, but I saw someone."

"Who?"

"A burglar."

"How do you know he was a burglar?" I asked.

"Well," said Billy, "he was climbing up the side of one of those old houses on Quiet Street. I landed on the roof of a house opposite and watched."

"Climbing up a ladder, you mean?"

"No, he was climbing up the ivy on the wall, and when he got to an upstairs window he opened it with something and slipped inside."

"A cat burglar!" Lilyleaf said.

"Oh, wow!" said Billy.

"Oh, no!" I said. "Oh, Lilyleaf, what if he breaks into our house and steals you!"

"No," she said. "A cat burglar is someone who is very nimble and agile and stealthy and clever and good at climbing up things. Just like a cat."

I wonder if it'll be in the evening newspaper, I thought the next day. Later I sneaked a look at

Dad's copy while he was watching the TV. The headline said:

YET ANOTHER DARING ROBBERY!

The latest in what is now a long line of burglaries occurred in the early hours of this morning. An intruder broke in through an upper window at 22 Quiet Street and stole a quantity of jewelry without disturbing the members of the household. As with previous thefts, no ladder appears to have been used and it is presumed that the man climbed the ivy on the house wall in the classic manner of cat burglars.

Only then did I remember that our house walls are covered with ivy!

Six

At breakfast I said to Dad, "Did you see that article in last night's paper? About the burglar?"

"Yes," he said.

"Well, our house is covered with ivy. He might climb up our walls next. He could, easy, he's a cat burglar."

Dad laughed.

"Afraid he'll steal Lilyleaf?" he said. "I wouldn't worry too much about it, Mary, especially just now. With all my Christmas lights, ours is the most brightly lit house in town, I think. Anyone would be able to see a cat burglar climbing up our walls."

He got up from the table.

"I'll be a bit late coming home this evening," he said to Mom. "I have the usual Monday meeting of the Ways and Means Committee, and I'm in the chair."

When he'd gone off to work I said to Mom, "What do people do at a meeting?"

"Oh, they talk about things."

"What are 'ways and means'?"

"Oh, how to do things."

"What did Dad mean—he's going to be in the chair. Do all the others have to stand up?"

"You and your endless questions, Mary!" Mom said. "It means he's the chairman; he's in charge of the meeting."

When I got back from school that Monday afternoon, I said to Lilyleaf, "We're going to have a meeting. In the living room." I went down the garden to get Mr. Keylock from his hutch and told him.

"Eating, did you say?" he asked.

"No," I said. "Meeting."

I came back and sat in Dad's big armchair. Billy was watching TV and Mom was busy in the kitchen. The guinea pig sat on my lap, and the cat lay along the arm of the chair.

"Okay," I said to them, "this is a meeting of the Ways and Means Committee. I'm in the chair."

"Any fool can see that," said Mr. Keylock in a grumpy voice, "but I haven't had my dinner."

"Ways and means of what?" Lilyleaf said.

"Of protecting this house against that cat burglar."

Mr. Keylock didn't exactly prick up his ears (he can't), but he said, "He doesn't steal guinea pigs, does he?"

"No, nor cats. But he steals jewelry and stuff, and he does climb like a cat. Billy saw him last night. What I'm asking this committee is, how do we find ways and means of guarding against him? Mr. Keylock?"

"No good asking me," said the guinea pig. "I sleep at night, like all sensible creatures."

"I don't," said Lilyleaf, "and I'm also more sensible than some I could mention. I can be on patrol outside."

"But how would you give warning?" I said.

"Make a terrible horrible awful racket, I suppose," said Lilyleaf. "It's a pity that Billy only flies once a month. He'd be the ideal guard. Just imagine, that old burglar would have forty fits if he suddenly saw Billy the Bird."

Mom came in.

"Dinner's nearly ready," she said to me.

"I wish mine was," squeaked Mr. Keylock.

To Billy, Mom said, "Turn that thing off."

"But it's the Teletubbies," he said.

"Well, turn it off as soon as it's over," she said, and turned to me. "Have you done your homework?"

"No," I said. "We've been having a meeting. I'm in the chair."

"You're a funny girl," said Mom. "You jabber away to those two animals as though they could understand what you mean. Dinner in ten minutes." She went out of the room.

Mr. Keylock started to chatter angrily and Lilyleaf began to purr loudly, and it was easy enough for me to understand what they meant. The guinea pig was annoyed because he hadn't eaten, and the cat was amused because the guinea pig was annoyed. As for me, I was worried because the meeting of the Ways and Means Committee hadn't gotten us anywhere.

"I'm worried," I said to Lilyleaf that night. She was lying on my bed as she often did before going downstairs and through the cat door for a night's hunting.

She got up and stretched and rubbed her furry face against mine, purring softly as if to say, "Don't worry, it may never happen." And in fact it didn't. Christmas came and went, and Dad took down the Christmas lights, and the new year began. Perhaps the cat burglar was too busy enjoying himself, thanks to all the valuable things he must have stolen, but there had been no more reports of thefts by the time the January full moon rose. I wondered if he'd moved on to another neighborhood.

Once again Billy slept later than he had at the summer and autumn full moons, and it was after midnight when Lilyleaf went "Pssst" in my ear before going off on patrol. I raced to Billy's room and found him zipping around the ceiling.

"Listen, Billy," I said to him when I had him dressed and ready for takeoff. "Fly along above as many streets in the town as you can, especially where there are houses with ivy or Virginia creeper on them, and see if you can spot that burglar again. Stealing things is wrong. He should be stopped."

"What do I do if I see him?" Billy asked.

"Make a terrible horrible awful racket," I said, "to wake people up. But don't let them see you. Fly straight home."

"Okay," said my little brother, grinning, as I opened the window.

"Watch out, burglar! Here comes Billy the Bird!"

Seven

When he'd flown away, I shut the window and sat in a chair beside it, ready to let him in again when he returned. With no Lilyleaf to wake me—she was on patrol outside—of course I fell asleep.

I was suddenly woken by not one but two terrible horrible ghastly noises. One came from Lilyleaf, caterwauling in the street below, and the other seemed to be just above the bedroom window. I opened it and looked out, to see a sight I will never forget. Nor more than six feet below me, under the window, clinging to the ivy, was the figure of a man dressed all in black and wearing a black hood.

I looked upward, and there above the window hovered Billy, making hideous faces, sticking his fingers in his ears, poking his tongue out, crossing his eyes, and letting out the weirdest noises, like "Ah! Wah! Gah! Gummygummygummy! Wollywollywoo!"

Then, louder even than boy or cat, the man let out a great yell of terror, lost his grip on the ivy, and fell, landing on our lawn with a horrible thump.

"Come in, quick, Billy," I called, and then I shut the window, pulled off the extra clothes he was wearing, and popped him into bed and scuttled off to my own room.

I lay there, hearing Dad and Mom go rushing down the stairs, and then came the noise of a lot of people talking excitedly outside. Last came the *Nee naw! Nee naw!* of sirens, first a police car and then an ambulance.

I got up and went and looked in Billy's room,

but he was sound asleep despite all the rumpus, so I went downstairs, too.

"What's happening?" I said to Mom and Dad, who were standing on the lawn in their pajamas, talking to our neighbors.

"It's that cat burglar, Mary," Dad said.

"He must have been climbing up our wall and fallen off," Mom said.

"They're just loading him into the ambulance," said Dad.

"Come on, Mary," said Mom. "Back to bed." She came upstairs with me and went on into Billy's room.

"Can you believe it!" she said when she came back. "He slept right through all that terrible horrible ghastly racket! Never knew anything about it! You go back to sleep. There's a good girl." Before I did, Lilyleaf came in and jumped up on my bed, purring like mad.

"A good night's work," she said. "I think I'll have a catnap."

When I woke up next morning, I lay in bed imagining another conversation.

MARY: Billy *did* know about it.

MOM: How could he? It didn't even wake him.

MARY: He was awake all right. Long before the noise woke you up. He frightened the cat burglar so much that he fell off the ivy.

DAD: What do you mean?

MARY: Well, he hovered right above the man, making faces and awful noises.

DAD: What d'you mean, he hovered?

MARY: I told you before. He can fly. Like a bird.

DAD AND MOM TOGETHER (GETTING ANGRY): Oh, Mary. Don't be silly. You have such an imagination!

Tuesday evening's newspaper reported:

CAT BURGLAR ARRESTED

In the early hours of this morning, an attempted robbery by the town's now notorious cat burglar ended in his fall from the ivy-covered wall he had been climbing. He was taken by ambulance to the Main Hospital, where he was found to be suffering from a concussion, though otherwise miraculously unhurt. Police are at his bedside.

But Wednesday's report was much fuller:

CAT BURGLAR
ATTACKED BY ALIEN

The intruder who fell from the wall of a house yesterday has now told police that he was attacked by a space alien. He described his attacker as a monstrous thing the size of a small boy. It had its thumbs in its ears and its tongue stuck out from a hideous face, as he could clearly see by the light of the full moon. It flew down out of the night sky, he stated, and hovered above him, cursing him in a foreign language.

Could this be connected with the UFO that was supposedly sighted on September 16 last year? Or was the man's story simply the result of a concussion? Throughout, he insisted that the alien was definitely flying. The man has now been taken into custody.

I told Lilyleaf about the articles in the paper.

"He was lucky not to break his neck," she said. "Perhaps cat burglars have nine lives."

I told Mr. Keylock, but as usual he only wanted to talk about food. I told Billy the Bird. (He hadn't read the newspaper, of course—he can't read.)

"Wow!" he said. "An alien! I wish I'd seen the man fall off the wall!"

You did, Billy, I said to myself. You did.

Eight

"I had an idea," I said to Lilyleaf and Mr. Keylock. It was Saturday morning, and I was cleaning out the guinea pig's hutch as I always do then. He groans and grumbles because it means he has to wait longer than usual for his breakfast. Lilyleaf usually comes to watch, wearing an expression that says plainly that it's a pity other animals aren't as clean in their habits as cats are.

"An idea about what?" she said.

"About Billy's next scheduled flight, in February," I replied.

"What idea?" said Mr. Keylock. "And hurry up, girl, I'm famished."

"Well," I said, "we don't really know where he goes or what he does on these flights. Except for the last one. Usually when he returns, he just goes straight to sleep and then of course the next day he doesn't even know he's been flying. If only I could go on a flight with him—but of course he couldn't carry me, I'm much too heavy."

"So am I," said Lilyleaf quickly.

"But aren't you curious to find out what flying would be like?" I said to her.

"Curiosity killed the cat," she replied. "But you never know, guinea pigs might fly." We both turned to Mr. Keylock.

"Don't look at me!" he squeaked.

"You don't weigh much," I said to him. "Billy could easily carry you."

"Billy could easily drop me!" said Mr. Keylock.

After I'd put fresh sawdust on his hutch floor and filled his hayrack and his water bottle and given him some cabbage leaves, Lilyleaf and I walked back through the yard together.

"How long do you suppose Billy will go on flying?" I asked her. "You don't think he'll still be doing it when he's bigger? He'll get too heavy to lift off, won't he?"

"Think of those astronauts," the cat said (she'd seen them on TV, too). "They're weightless, no matter how big they really are."

"So he could still be doing it when he's a grown man as big as Dad?" I asked.

Lilyleaf made a sort of chuckling noise and then I began to giggle. Dad is a very big man, a little on the fat side, to be honest, and I had a sudden mental picture of him swooping and soaring above the town like a jumbo jet. How horrified the townspeople would be if they saw the large figure of the Chairman of the Ways and Means Committee whizzing over their heads!

"Sooner or later somebody's bound to spot him," I said. "Close enough to see that what they're looking at isn't a UFO or an alien, but a small boy called Bird, flying like one. Then all the world would come to our town, prime ministers and presidents and pop stars, even queens and kings perhaps, to see this flying boy, and it'd be in all the newspapers and on the TV and the radio and there'd be film crews everywhere and we'd never have a moment's peace."

None of that had happened as a result of the January flight, because no one had seen Billy except the cat burglar, and no one believed his story because they thought he was drunk or had had a concussion or was crazy. But our local evening paper went on and on about UFOs and aliens, printing letters from people who believed in one or the other.

He's much more likely to be seen now, I thought, because they'll be looking for him, looking up into skies lit by a full moon. But, luckily I suppose, the weather at the full moon was terrible both in February and in March, so that Billy had to be content with flying around indoors.

Not till the following month did I allow him to fly outdoors again.

Once again we worked it out so that he didn't take off till well after midnight, but the April full moon was the most brilliant one imaginable. The town was lit up as though by a great searchlight in the sky.

"Someone," I said to Lilyleaf, "is bound to see him this time." And someone did.

Boys will be boys, the saying goes, and Billy could be naughty or silly just as all little boys are now and then. I suppose he must have gotten bored with just flying quietly around and thought he'd amuse himself by giving someone a fright.

So he landed on top of the church tower and sat there, dangling his legs. He looked down, and there in the street right below him was a man, a man in uniform walking slowly along.

Billy couldn't have know it was a policeman

on his beat and probably wouldn't have cared anyway. He just thought, I suppose, that it would be fun to give this man a fright, so he shouted "BOO!" How do I know all this? Because it was all in next evening's paper.

FURTHER SIGHTING OF ALIEN?

Readers may remember the story that we printed about a burglar who, in January, stated that he had been attacked by an alien, a story that many of our readers considered to be nonsense. Now, however, a further sighting has occurred, this time from a much more reliable source. Our community policeman, Officer George Gibbs, made the following report.

"At 1:00 A.M. I was passing St. Margaret's Church when I heard a loud, shrill cry above me. Looking up, I could see clearly by the light of the full moon a figure sitting on the very top of the church tower. I was unable to distinguish its features, but it appeared to be the size of a small child about four years of age. How it came to be there, I had no idea, since the church is kept locked at night and no child could possibly have scaled the tower from the outside, but it was obviously in a position of the gravest danger.

"Don't move!" I called up to it. "Just stay right where you are. Help is on its way," and I called the police station on my walkie-talkie. I requested them to summon the fire brigade, which apparatus arrived at St. Margaret's Church at 1:17 A.M."

As soon as the fire engine arrived, the firemen extended a long ladder to the top of the church tower where the figure was still sitting. While one fireman climbed the ladder, the others called up to the figure to stay put. However, it then disappeared, presumably moving down the other side.

But when a fireman reached the head of the ladder, the newspaper report went on to say, and climbed up the steep roof to the top of the tower, he found that it was empty. There was no sign of anyone, and a search of the interior of the church and of the churchyard revealed nothing.

Finally, the report concluded:

Whatever Officer Gibbs had seen on top of St. Margaret's Church had vanished into thin air. How can it have done this, human or alien, unless it had the power of flight? Humans do not have this power. Aliens presumably do.

Nine

I looked up the date of the May full moon. As usual, it was represented in my diary, under the date, by a circle like a capital O, like this:

O—Full moon.

I did happen to notice that on this particular date in May it read:

O—Full moon

and then, in parentheses:

(Lunar eclipse)

I had no idea what those last two words meant, so I didn't mention them to Lilyleaf. In fact I never thought about them till the actual night. It was a warm one, and Billy flew off after midnight in his blue pajamas with the pattern of pink rabbits.

I stood at the window in the brilliant moonlight, looking at that great round circle in the sky and the pattern of darker marks on its white surface. Some people think of it as the face of a man—the Man in the Moon. Some people swear they can see on it the outline of a rabbit.

As I stared at it, I noticed a curious shadow starting to appear at the lower rim of the circle, as though a curved dark cloud were beginning to intrude upon the moon's brightness.

I tried to keep on watching, because the shadow seemed to be getting bigger, while the moon's light grew fainter. But I just couldn't stay awake, until the usual "Pssst" woke me. I looked out and saw that only about a quarter of the face of the moon was still showing.

"What's happening?" I asked Lilyleaf.

"Didn't it say, in your diary?" she said.

"Say what?"

"That tonight's the night of a lunar eclipse."

"Oh," I said. "Oh yes, but I didn't know what it meant."

"It means," said the cat, "that now and again the moon enters the earth's shadow. Then, before long, that shadow spreads right over the face of the moon and blots it out."

"Blots out its light, you mean? But then how will Billy see to fly back?"

"Let us just hope," said Lilyleaf, "that he is able to fly back. Better open that window, ready."

Just then we heard a sort of thump on the wall outside. It couldn't be that cat burglar, could it, I thought? They locked him up, didn't they?

I looked out and leaned over, and there, clinging to the ivy just below the window, was my little brother.

"Mary, Mary! Help me!" he cried. I stretched down and grabbed his arms and somehow

managed to pull him up over the windowsill and into his bedroom.

"Whatever's happened?" I said. "Why didn't you just fly in?"

"I couldn't," Billy said. "I was flying really, really high and then it began to get darker and I began to come down, lower and lower, I couldn't help it, and I got so tired I thought I was going to crash-land, but I just managed to cross the lawn and I got nearly up to the window. But then I felt I couldn't fly anymore and I grabbed hold of the ivy."

He yawned enormously.

"Help me into bed, Mary," he said, and I did, and immediately he fell asleep.

Before I went to my own room, I looked out of Billy's window and saw the last thin gleam of that May full moon disappear, completely covered now, in the lunar eclipse.

All was pitch-dark.

In the morning Billy of course remembered

nothing about the drama of the night. Mom and Dad knew nothing about it either. At breakfast Dad opened his daily newspaper and said to Mom, "Hey! There was an eclipse of the moon last night!"

"I didn't know that," Mom said.

"I didn't know that," Mr. Keylock said when I told him.

"Billy started to lose his power of weightlessness," I explained, "because of the full moon being covered over. He was lucky not to have crashed."

Just then Billy came through the yard carrying a dandelion, which he gave to the guinea pig.

Mr. Keylock twiddled his red mustache.

"You're a good boy," he said. "Even if you never become weightless again."

"What does he mean?" asked Billy, as we walked back through the yard.

"You don't remember, do you?" I said. "Having such a hard time getting home? Because of the eclipse?"

"Eclipse?" said my little brother. "What are you talking about, Mary?"

I sighed. At least you won't miss flying, I thought, because you've never known you can. But I will be very sorry if you've lost your powers.

"Do you think he has?" I asked Lilyleaf later.

"Do I think who has what?"

"Billy. Lost his powers of weightlessness. Because of the lunar eclipse. Or do you think that on the next full moon he'll be flying again?"

"We can only wait and see," said Lilyleaf, "but something tells me that your brother may now be grounded, permanently."

And sadly she was right.

The moon waxed and the moon waned, month by month, but never again, when it was full, did Billy the Bird defy gravity.

Perhaps it wasn't anything to do with the eclipse, perhaps he'd just grown out of it, but on every date where my diary recorded "O—Full moon" I kept watch in the evening and Lilyleaf kept watch all through the night, keeping guard over my little brother, waiting for him to levitate, to rise, just a few inches perhaps, a few feet, up to the ceiling maybe, the way he had that first time.

But he never moved.

"It's no good for me to tell him everything that has happened," I said to Lilyleaf. "He just says I've been dreaming, or thinks I'm crazy. Only you and I know the truth. You and I and Mr. Keylock."

"And the old cat burglar," said the old cat.

One evening the following summer, in June, almost exactly two years after Billy's maiden flight, we were all sitting on the swing seat on the lawn, enjoying the evening sunshine—Mom and Dad and Billy and me and Lilyleaf and Mr. Keylock.

It was late, well past Billy's bedtime, but it was such a lovely evening that he had been allowed to stay up.

Suddenly we saw a pale ghostly shape floating across our garden.

"Look!" said Dad. "An owl."

"Oh!" said Mom. "Wouldn't it be wonderful to be able to fly like that!"

"Wouldn't it," said Dad.

"It would," I said.

Lilyleaf began to purr and Mr. Keylock gave a grunt.

"People can't fly," my little brother said.

"You're right, Billy," Dad replied. "Because of the force of gravity. People could only fly if they were weightless. Like astronauts in a spacecraft, in orbit beyond Earth's atmosphere."

"I dreamed," I said, and I squeezed Mr. Keylock and nudged Lilyleaf, "I dreamed that Billy could fly." (And as I said it, I wondered for an instant, had I dreamed it all?)

"Me? Fly? Don't be so silly, Mary," said Billy the Bird.

But I haven't given up hope, mostly because of

something that wise old Lilyleaf said to me that very night.

I was lying in bed, thinking about all the adventures of my little brother Billy the Bird, when the cat came in and jumped up beside me.

I stroked her and she purred.

"He's never going to fly again, is he?" I said.

"No," said Lilyleaf. "He's earthbound. That lunar eclipse eclipsed his magic powers. But I've thinking about it, and it seems quite possible to me that in years to come, when Billy is grown up and marries and becomes a father, he may perhaps pass on those powers to his child. His son or his daughter might inherit them, just the way you've inherited your mom's blue eyes and Mr. Keylock, no doubt, his father's red mustache."

"So that one day in the future," I said, "there could be another flying Bird!"

DICK KING-SMITH was born and raised in Gloucestershire, England. Growing up, he had many favorite pet animals. After working as a farmer for twenty years, he became a teacher and a children's book author.

Pigs are Dick King-Smith's favorite animals, and he often writes about these special creatures. He loves all animals, and most of all, he loves to write what he calls farmyard fantasy for children. He also enjoys meeting the children who read his books and knowing that they really enjoy what he does.

Among his many well-known books is *Babe: The Gallant Pig*, which was made into a major motion picture and was nominated for an Academy Award.

Dick King-Smith lives with his wife in a small seventeenth-century cottage, about three miles from the house where he was born.